For Malik – A. H. Benjamin
For Finn & Tilly, with love x – Nick East

Editor: Ruth Symons
Designer: Bianca Lucas
Managing Editor: Victoria Garrard
Design Manager: Anna Lubecka

Copyright © QED Publishing 2013

First published in the UK in 2013 by QED Publishing
A Quarto Group company, The Old Brewery
6 Blundell Street, London, N7 9BH

www.qed-publishing.co.uk

A catalogue record for this book is available from the British Library.

ISBN 978 1 78171 135 4

Printed in China

IN A MINUTE, MUM

A. H. Benjamin
and Nick East

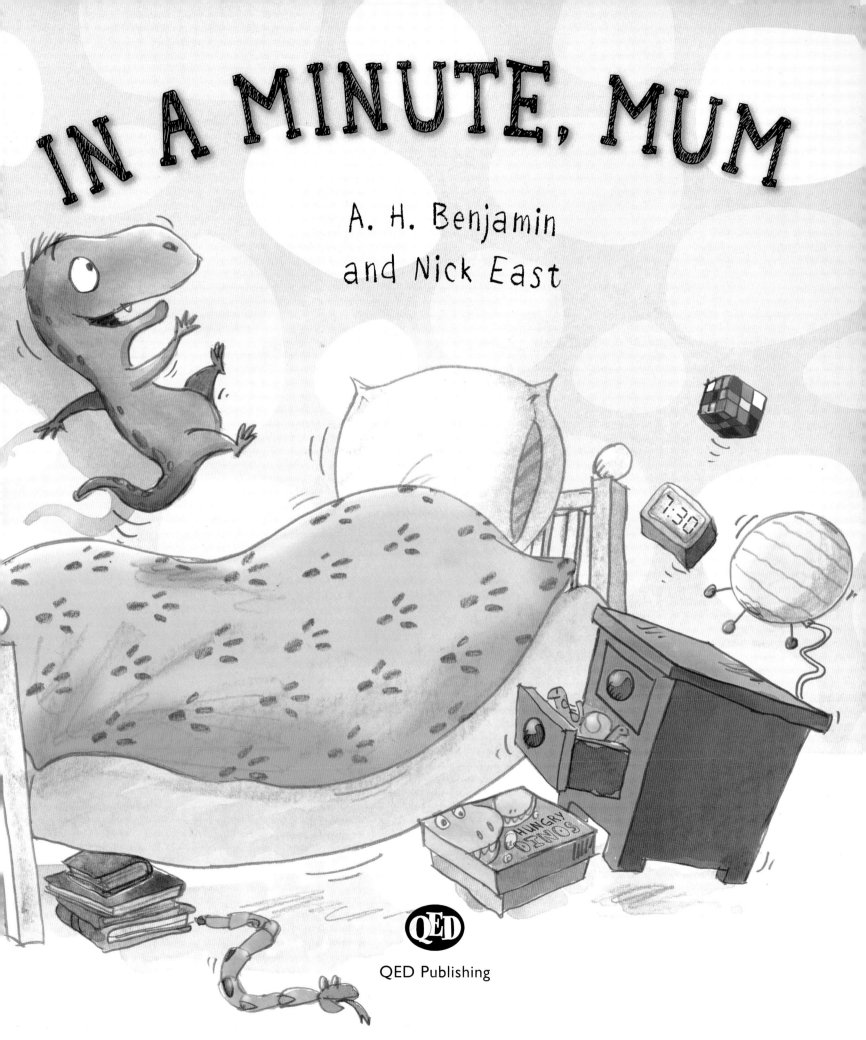

QED

QED Publishing

Mum was busy baking.

"It looks like rain," she said.
"Please can you bring in the
washing, Rory?"

"In a minute, Mum..." Rory said.
He was busy eating a snack.

Fifteen minutes later, it started raining.
The clothes on the line were soaked.

"Oh, Rory!" said Mum.

Dad was working in the garage.

"Please can you pick up my newspaper, Rory?" he asked.

"In a minute..." Rory said. He was busy playing.

Half an hour later, Rory went to the shop – but it had closed!

"Oh, Rory," grumbled Dad.

Rory's big sister Tina was finishing her homework.

"Please can you turn off my bath, Rory?" she asked.

"In a minute..." Rory said.
He was busy watching TV.

Ten minutes later the bathroom was flooded.
"Oh, Rory!" cried Tina.

On the way to school Rory stopped to look in a toy shop window.

"Come on," said his friend, Terry. "We'll be late!"

"In a minute..." Rory said. He was busy looking at the toys.

£30

£90

DINO BRIX

£25

£15

£15

BOX-A-SAURS

The teacher told them off for being late.
"It's your fault, Rory," mumbled Terry.

Everybody was fed up with Rory.

"He always puts things off," said Dad.

"And he's always late," said Mum.

"He's **impossible!**" agreed Tina.

They decided something had to be done...

Rory was hungry after playing football all afternoon.

"Can you make me a sandwich, Mum?" he asked.

"In a minute..." Mum said. She carried on watching TV.

Rory went hungry until dinner time.

Rory wanted to go for a bike ride with his friends, but his bike had a flat tyre.

"Can you fix it, Dad?" asked Rory.

"In a minute..." Dad said.
He carried on reading his newspaper.

Rory sulked when his friends left without him.

Rory needed the toilet,
but Tina was in the bathroom.

"Are you coming out?"
Rory called.

"In a minute..." Tina said. She kept on singing in the shower.

Rory had to keep his legs crossed for a long time.

"Everyone keeps making me wait!" Rory cried.
"Now you know how it feels," said Mum.

Mum thought it would help to buy Rory a watch.

Rory watched as the second hand ticked its way around.

Tick Tock!

"A minute's not long at all!" said Rory.

"I'm sorry, I didn't realize I was taking so long."

"Will you show me your new watch?" asked Tina.

"In a min–" began Rory, but then he stopped.
"Oh, okay," he grinned.

Next steps

After reading the story, look at the front cover again. What did the children think the book was about before they read it? What made them think that?

Rory keeps saying "in a minute" to his family. Ask the children to count how many times this phrase is repeated.

In the story, Rory is always putting things off. Ask the children if they have ever put off an important task. Did this get them into trouble? How did it make them feel?

Rory's family ask him to help with everyday tasks. Ask the children if they ever help with household chores. What do they do?

Do the children know what a minute is? How many seconds are there in a minute? Do they know how to tell the time?

What type of creature is Rory? Can the children name different types of dinosaur? Ask the children to draw themselves and their families as dinosaurs. What sort of dinosaur would they want to be?